IN HIS OWN WORDS:

Colin Powell

D0031964

IN HIS OWN WORDS:

Colin Powell

Edited and Collected by

Lisa Shaw

A PERIGEE BOOK

A Perigee Book
Published by The Berkley Publishing Group
200 Madison Avenue
New York, NY 10016

Copyright © 1995 by Lisa Shaw
Book design by Jill Dinneen
Cover design by Altitude Graphic Design
Cover photo by AP/World Wide Photos/Mike Fisher; used by
permission.

The sources for the quotations that appear in this book can be
found in the back of the book, beginning on page 137.

First edition: December 1995
ISBN: 0-399-52224-7

Published simultaneously in Canada.

The Putnam Berkley World Wide Web site address is
http://www.berkley.com

Printed in the United States of America

10 9 8 7 6 5 4 3 2 1

For my husband, Dan

Introduction

Who is General Colin Luther Powell? And what does he stand for?

With the publication of his memoirs, *My American Journey*, the speculation in the media and among a majority of Americans who are dissatisfied with the political scene today and are curious about the political ambitions of Powell has reached a fever pitch. The general consensus has been that Powell hasn't been forthcoming about how he feels about certain issues that concern us all, from abortion to welfare.

When I first began to research this book, I was prepared to dig deep for information about what this popular non-candidate believes and says. What I found, however, was a different story. There's a wealth of information and straight-from-the-horse's-mouth quotes from General Powell that show exactly where he stands on the issues. And they're all right here in this book.

Like many Americans, I'm disillusioned with the state of American politics today. Especially since I live in New Hampshire, where the candidates have been tramping across the state for two years now, throwing on red flannel shirts, chowing down on barbecued chicken, and basically telling us the same things we've heard for years—and have learned to tune out.

Powell is different. For one, he sounds like a real person, not a special-interest maven. Second, the mystery of Powell has set us all afire. And third, he simply sounds too good to be true.

So use this book to get an idea of where Powell stands on the issues. You'll also discover his great talent for storytelling as well as a wit that has been long missing from the American political scene. Whether or not he decides to run for president in 1996, knowing his views will allow you to hope that if not '96, there's always the year 2000. . . .

—Lisa Shaw

IN HIS OWN WORDS:

Colin Powell

The past two years I've done no interviews, no television. People are wondering what Forrest Gump Colin Powell stands for. Well, they're about to find out, as I deal with the various issues that are out there and I become a public figure again.

On Politics

A Kabuki dance. *(Powell on Washington)*

♦

I tell people that I'm not a professional politician. . . . I don't find a passion for politics. I don't find that I have that calling for politics. But I want to keep the option open.

Now people say, 'But Powell knows nothing about politics. As soon as he talks about all entitlements, he's just touched the third rail of American political life.' Well good, I'm glad I touched it, because the American people cannot continue to be deceived the way they are, that somehow you can set aside 40 to 50 percent of the budget and never look at it. I would look at the whole package and try to bring it in balance, and if you could do that without raising taxes, that's fine.

♦

I'm not sure anyone or anything can live up to the standards the American people are trying to put on their political process, because politics is ultimately debate, fighting, compromise, consensus, and then you get the synthesis you need to move forward. But it isn't always pretty to watch.

♦

On Whether He's a Republican or a Democrat

Even after working two years in the West Wing,
there isn't a single one of my White House
friends from those days who could tell you today
whether they think I'm a Republican or a
Democrat. That was part of the code I lived
with. Now I'm no longer protected by my
uniform. As I go around the country, I'm trying
to develop a political philosophy, just to be a
good citizen, not necessarily to run for office.

♦

Active duty military officers have no business talking about partisan political matters. So nobody knows what party I belong to or don't belong to or may belong to. This is the way it should be.

◆

You don't know my politics. Nobody does.

◆

Republican consultant David Welch: "I'm working on Colin—he's a Republican."
Commerce Secretary Ron Brown: "No, man, he's on our side."
Powell: "I'm getting out of here."

◆

I'm certainly more moderate in my views than most of the more active Republicans who are out there right now fighting for the heart and soul of the party.

◆

I have pretty much ruled out the Democrats. . . . I have no particular enthusiasm for the Democratic Party or the positions it stands for.

◆

It's important for me to have something that I believe in, rather than try to make my beliefs fit a party just for the purpose of saying I belong to it.

I have very strong Republican leanings on
economic and foreign-policy matters, but I was a
New Deal kid. I had pictures of Franklin
Roosevelt on my wall.

◆

If the Republicans knew my views on domestic
policy, I'm not sure they would like me so
much.

◆

I will not dodge this question, I will answer it
right back, straightforwardly: I am neither.

◆

You know, I'm sort of a liberal guy, up to this point, but here's where I become a Republican: once these kids come out of school, there has got to be a capitalistic entrepreneurial system that is just burning up the place to create the jobs for these kids. And therefore you've got to get the tax burden off business. You've got to lower the capital-gains tax.

◆

My entire code of honor said, Don't be political, never show any partisanship, either Democratic or Republican.

◆

No party has really lost its core, core constituents before. Many black [Democratic] congressmen have said to me, 'If you come out, I can't go nowhere. Go out and campaign against you? That'd be crazy.' They can't. They won't. A number of them have said, 'You know we'll campaign for you wherever you are.'

♦

The question comes up all the time, and I have been religious with respect to the answer to that question.

♦

[Italian Prime Minister Lamberto Dini] was trying to form a government on his claim to fame that he belongs to no political party. He is absolutely apolitical. . . . And he's been selected to form a government on that basis. Interesting!

◆

It's hard to redefine or create a new center in a couple of months. I could do it in four years.

◆

Neither of the two major parties fits me comfortably in its present state.

◆

The weather is beautiful. *(His response to a reporter's question about his political affiliation)*

[The Democrats] don't have the same intellectual firmament, they're not alive and well like the Republican Party is.

♦

If I were to decide to enter politics and run for the presidency, the easiest way to do it, I think, would be as a Republican. It would probably be more of an issue of me making compromises than it would be for the Republican Party making compromises, if we're talking about 1995–96.

On His Net Worth

I'm now a wealthy person. I wasn't wealthy when I retired. I mean, I just figured out what the white guys were doing.

What have I done with my wealth? I bought my wife a nice house, I bought two new suits, leased a new car. What have I done with the rest of it? Invested it. Some of it is in bonds. Where's that bond money going? It's building things—cities. Some of it is in the equity market. What's it doing? It's financing companies. It's looking for more places to create wealth, and guess what happens when that happens. Jobs are going to be created.

On School

In our schools, we must teach our children that alone it is difficult to accomplish things but that together, as a team, as a family, almost anything can be accomplished.

If you don't get that high-school diploma, you're on your way to nowhere. . . . In fact, you probably can't even get into my Army these days. . . . [It shows that] somebody will stick to the task given. It shows that you can overcome obstacles.

♦

In our schools, we must have discipline and we must have high standards. To enforce that, we must have a working system of rewards and punishments—a *working* system, not a paper system, and not a system simply to satisfy a bureaucracy.

♦

On the Current Slate of Republican Presidential Candidates

Philosophically, the [Republican] party is wider than you might expect just from listening to the ordinary rhetoric. There are a lot of Republicans who are somewhat silent and tend to be more in the moderate, Rockefeller vein. In order to appeal to the active wing of the party, most candidates are tacking to the right, and that seems to be what Bob Dole is doing.

♦

When I look at the other candidates who are out there, they have had a lifelong ambition to rise in politics; they have been doing it all their lives. And to them the Holy Grail is the presidency. That has not been my driving ambition.

On the Role of Government

The government's got to get off people's backs. They've got to have minimum regulations, for safety and for some level of security, so we're not plundering things. But after that, get off their backs.

♦

Don't expect Washington to solve it. Don't expect the Left or the Right to solve it, or politicians to solve it. Ultimately, it will be solved by each and every one of us participating in community work as members of school boards or whatever else you may do in your community.

On School Prayer

I think prayer belongs, first and foremost, in the home. But I have no problem, if, on arriving at school, a quiet moment is allowed for a child to do whatever a child wishes to do in that private moment. I would be against any sort of stricture that says you will come in and you will pray and anything of that nature, and I don't think that's what most people have in mind.

On Abortion

I believe that we should do a lot more to teach young people to avoid pregnancy. I believe that a child should be a product of two people who are in love and prepared to nurture and care for that child. If a woman becomes pregnant and does not wish the child, I hope she would carry the child to term and then put the child up for adoption. If, however, it is her choice to abort, that's a matter between her, her doctor, her family and her conscience and her God, and if she chooses to abort, that's her choice. So that's pro-choice.

◆

I would counsel [a daughter of a friend who wanted to get an abortion] to think it through very carefully because she has participated in an act that has left her carrying a fetus that is alive. . . . So I would ask her to give some serious consideration to carrying the child to term and delivering it for adoption. But it's her body. It's her life. . . . I think that it is a choice that she must be free to make.

On Civilian Life

One of the saddest figures in all Christendom is the Chairman of the Joint Chiefs of Staff, once removed, driving around with a baseball cap pulled over his eyes, making his strategic choice as to whether it's going to be McDonald's or Taco Bell.

On Race in America

How did I deal with racism? I beat it. I said, 'I
am not going to carry this burden of racism. I'm
going to destroy your stereotype.' I'm proud to
be black. You carry this burden of racism,
because I'm not going to.

◆

I tell young blacks that even more is expected of
you. Don't let your blackness, your minority
status, be a problem to you. . . . Don't use it as
an excuse for your own shortcomings.

◆

African Americans start the game with a strike or two against us. We cannot afford to neglect any field of education or any effort at education.

♦

I want you to respect one another, see the best in each other, share each other's pain and joy. I want you to fight racism. I want you to rail against it. We have to make sure that it bleeds to death in this country once and for all.

♦

When people say to me, 'Weren't you held back?' and 'Don't people look at you funny?' and 'Don't they think you really aren't as important as you are because you're black?' my simple answer is, 'My color is somebody else's problem and not mine. You just take me as I am.'

I can't go so far as to become the leader of the civil rights movement in my position, but I never leave any doubt in anyone's mind that there's a lot more to be done.

◆

Many interviewers, when they come to talk to me, think they're being progressive by not mentioning in their stories any longer that I'm black. I tell them, 'Don't stop now. If I shot somebody, you'd have mentioned it. Fifty-three years you've been saying it. Don't stop now.'

◆

What my color is is somebody else's problem, not mine. People will say, 'You're a terrific black general.' I'm trying to be the best *general* I can be.

I was lucky to be born black. *(Remarking to a friend in 1972 when he became a White House Fellow)*

◆

My race has probably helped me more than it's hurt me.

◆

I can remember very well being denied access to a lunch counter. This isn't ancient . . . there are still racial problems in our country.

◆

I completely identified with the [civil rights]
struggle [in 1963]. Because of my position and
the things I was doing in my career, in my life,
I didn't have a chance to participate in that
struggle in any active way. I did it my own way
by my own example and by helping other
people who were coming along as best I could,
but you better believe that I identified with that
struggle and continue to identify with that
struggle.

♦

I don't shove [race] in their face, you know? I
don't bring any stereotypes or threatening visage
to their presence. Some black people do. I can
overcome any stereotypes or reservations they
have, because I perform well. [And] *I ain't that
black*.

It is a racist society. All you have to do is listen to a Mark Fuhrman and you have to be concerned.

♦

While I had been fighting in Vietnam alongside brave soldiers trying to preserve their freedom, in my own land a long-simmering conflict had turned into an open fight in our streets and cities—a fight that had to be won.

♦

I can give you experiences out of my own life and I'm not talking about ancient experiences, I'm talking about recent experiences where there is a difference.

I remember some of those old-fashioned
traditional American values and do not wish to
see them return.

♦

Martin [Luther King]'s vision was that the day
would come when all Americans would someday
sit together at the table of brotherhood. . . . We
are not there yet.

♦

I speak reasonably well, like a white person. I
am very comfortable in a white social situation,
and I don't go off into a corner. My features are
clearly black, and I've never denied what I am.
It fits into their general social setting, so they do
not find me threatening.

I have been thrown out of hot dog stands in Georgia when I was a young captain just coming home from a year in Vietnam.

♦

The way I deal with it is, 'I'm going to beat you. I don't care what you think of me; I don't care what you think about my background or whether I'm black, I'm white, I'm yellow. You're going to have to beat me, as they say in basketball, in my face.'

♦

I was helped by the sacrifices of a lot of great guys who went before me, who led the charge, but did not benefit from the results of that work.

Go ask the rest of institutional and corporate America, ask them why they have not learned from the Tuskegee Airmen and our black Desert Storm heroes that men and women of color can do anything if they are given the opportunity, the training.

♦

I didn't know I was a minority.

♦

On His Parents

I've learned more about their early years in the
United States in recent years. As my name has
become a little more familiar around the
countryside, people have said, 'I remember that
family.' . . . People have sent me pictures of my
father taken when he was a very young man in
Connecticut. When he first arrived in the
country, he was working up there as day labor.

◆

[My mother] could cut me down with a single
glance.

◆

Until the day [my parents] died, I was never able to convince them that it would never be possible for me to do better than they did in providing their children with values and goals. . . . We didn't sit down at night like the Brady Bunch and review the work of the day. It was just the way they lived their lives.

♦

I finally decided that I had to see this place called 'home.' I visited all my ancestral homes [in Jamaica in 1961] in Top Hill and Mandeville, Spur Tree and Kingston, and had an absolutely wonderful time.

♦

In those days, when your parents expected something, it was what you had to do. In my family, especially, you did what your parents expected of you.

♦

[My mother] did piecework at home. My early memories are of watching her on Thursday night sitting at the kitchen table, bundling up all these little tags and putting rubber bands around them.

♦

My father came from a little lower down than my mother did. So he married a little above himself but not a whole lot. I mean, we're not talking about the Kennedys.

My mother was the laborer in the family and my father was the manager. My mother used to get even, because my father didn't finish high school and she did. Every now and then you would hear under her breath, 'Him who never finished high school.'

◆

There was something of a tradition of hard work being the way to succeed. And there was simply an expectation that existed in the family—you were supposed to do better. And it was a bloody disappointment to the family if you didn't.

◆

My parents were hard-working people. My father was gone all day, every day. He never came home before seven or eight at night. My mother came home tired, too.

♦

[My father] was only about five-three or five-four, a little man, but he was a patriarch because of his wisdom. He loved people. He would do anything to help them.

♦

On Being a West Indian Black

West Indians were never oppressed to the extent that Southern blacks were. Southern blacks were raised believing that they were inferior. . . . West Indians did not arrive in the United States thinking that way and, for the most part, they lived in the North, where it was different.

♦

Most West Indians are high Anglicans, the same as high Episcopalians—the higher the better. Their value system is a combination of the family and the British tradition, which was strong in Jamaica. They never forgot that they were British subjects. This makes them somewhat different from other American blacks.

On Heroism

Heroism isn't a conscious thought. It comes from caring about the people you're with.

On Family

We've got to teach our youngsters what a family means, what giving to your community means, what raising good children means. We've got to restore a sense of shame to our society. Nothing seems to shame us or outrage us anymore. We look at our television sets and see all kinds of trash, and we allow it to come into our homes. We're not ashamed of it anymore.

I credit most of [my success] to my family, a family that had expectations for the children of that family, for acquiring a fairly good education in the public school system and having a desire to get off the block.

♦

[Family] is the essence of what it is to be an American. We have to restore, in every school and every workplace, every office and every factory . . . that sense of family.

On America as a Family

We have to start thinking of America as a family. We have to stop screeching at each other, stop hurting each other, and instead start caring for, sacrificing for, and sharing with each other.

On the Proliferation of Gangs

What I do say is, how many middle-aged gang members do you know? Where do you think it leads? Where do you think not graduating high school leads? Where do you think drugs lead?

♦

On What He'd Do for the Inner City

I think I can serve as an example of what is possible and talk to the issue, encourage those of my fellow citizens who have done well not to walk away. . . . [But] anybody who thinks one person can come along as president and say 'I've got it'? It isn't going to happen. I'm very excited about that part of the Republican revolution that says stop looking to Washington, gang. Let's go back to a community-based society.

♦

You've got to start with the families, and then you've got to fix education so these little bright-eyed five-year-olds, who are innocent as the day is long and who know right from wrong, have all the education they need. And you have to do both these things simultaneously. It's like being able to support two military conflicts simultaneously.

◆

If you check my stats around here you'll find I've been to elementary schools, junior high schools, high schools trying to get the message out every way I can.

◆

On the Presidency

The American people are channel surfing. And you're going to channel surf in '96, '98, 2000, until you find something you like.

◆

I think I have the skills to handle the job.

◆

But I like to win. *(Powell's response to co-author Joseph E. Persico's statement that he should run for president because it would be "a noble cause")*

[It would be] easier to be president than to run for president. I'd rather be president than a presidential candidate.

◆

I really don't want to be elected to be the first black American president. I don't want to be the poster child for the brothers, or for guilty white liberals. That would not be true to the image I have of myself.

◆

[During my fellowship at the Office of Management and Budget] they asked me to head up a project to keep me out of trouble. . . . Nobody knew what happened to presidential orders when they gave them. Nixon was mad because he kept telling people to do things, and nothing would happen. So I tracked what happened to presidential directives . . . and for the first time we started capturing what the hell presidents ultimately do. It got me into every department, and that was very useful.

◆

Eisenhower was a person who could put together very interesting coalitions and be a natural war leader the people would respect. They saw Ike and they felt comfortable and confident. *I* like Ike.

Gifted political leadership is the ability to know how much the American people will let you do, plus a bit more.

On the Support People Show Him

I think you have to be brain dead not to take away a level of pressure from this, and a level of expectation.

♦

I would enter not to make a statement but to win. I understand the battlefield and I know what winning takes.

♦

The question is whether this is just popularity or political power. There's a difference.

You flatter me by saying 'You're the first guy who could ever really do it.' Well, isn't that, in and of itself, almost there?

◆

There are lots of people who might have a favorable view of me who would instantly have an unfavorable view as soon as I had to start taking domestic positions.

◆

You can't compare whatever ratings you get for me truly with the ratings of any other figure, because I'm somewhat shielded [from] the abuse and the hurly-burly and the tussle of normal political life.

On Being a Role Model

One of the most flattering things said about me is that I am a role model. That's a heck of a responsibility. Hopefully, I can be a role model for young blacks coming up, for all young Americans, one that says: 'Here's a guy that, even though he is black and his hair is kinky, has been rather successful. He's done a good job.'

◆

I'm sort of a crossover. I don't claim either to be a black leader or a white leader. I try to talk to all of America.

It's been enormously flattering to me to see the reaction from the black community. It's been a source of great pride to walk into a store and have a black man come up and say, 'I just wanted to shake your hand.' Or to drive through a parking lot . . . and have somebody chase me down to get a signature.

♦

On the American People

The American people are the smartest people on earth. I don't think they are captives of the evening news. When you leave this very intense center of the world in Washington and get out, you tend to find that they are able to absorb large amounts of information and pretty much come to a balanced conclusion, a fairly informed and well-balanced and rational conclusion about what they are seeing and what they are reading.

♦

You simply also have to have buried deep in your psyche the fact that the American people are not that patient. They like to see rather quick results whenever possible. . . . If you are going to conduct a military operation, try to do it in a way that gets it over quickly.

On Washington, D.C.

Ground Zero . . . GZ on the Potomac.

♦

I have been in a number of Washington
assignments, and I have never gone away saying,
'God, I hate the Pentagon. God, I hate the
White House.' . . . [But] you will not find me
having volunteered for any of these positions.
You can check with the people who hired me;
you'll find almost in every case I said I don't
want to do it.

◆

The whole thing is greased by compromise and
consensus.

On Military Reserves

The capabilities of the contingency and
expeditionary forces in the Army and Marine
Corps provide decisionmakers with valuable
alternatives and should be retained.

On Rap Music

It's not an artistry that I totally understand, but they are creative.

On the O.J. Verdict

People will try to suggest that because there were nine blacks on the jury, it was a racial judgment. I think that's unfair. These are people who can understand the facts put before them. They obviously believe that the facts did not support a conviction.

◆

On the Future

My simple message to you is, the only thing you
do with yesterday is learn from it . . . Save part
of today to prepare for tomorrow, and always be
thinking about the day after tomorrow, but
dream about next week.

◆

For the first time in the postwar generation,
there is hope throughout the world that we may
be in a new era of perhaps permanent peace
and prosperity.

◆

On the Process of Running for President

I can't sink to [the rough-and-tumble process] because it would be very inconsistent with who I am to go into a political campaign mode where I am slinging and fighting. I know how to counterpunch and I know how to take criticism and . . . how to deliver criticism. But I am not somebody who could go down into the mud and wallow around in it.

◆

On the Deep South in the Sixties

Even if you were a lieutenant in the United States Army, you knew better than to drink water in a place where you weren't supposed to or relieve yourself in a place where you weren't supposed to. You were bitter and you were mad, but you were an Army officer. The only contribution I could make was to knock down stereotypes with my performance.

♦

I wasn't even trying to do a sit-in. All I wanted was a hamburger. *(On being refused service in Columbus, Georgia, because he was black)*

On Charges That He Once Snubbed Someone

Well, I guess that out of the ten thousand people I meet a day, I didn't smile back at someone.

On His Childhood

What I realized after writing [the book] was that I was a well-taken-care-of, ordinary kid.

♦

What many people now call a slum was a
tenement neighborhood and a neat place to
grow up when I was a boy. . . . Every block
along 163rd Street had a repeating pattern to it.
There was always a Jewish bakery, a Puerto
Rican grocery, a Jewish candy store, a Chinese
laundry.

♦

I was always sort of a kid that had advantages
and disadvantages. One of the advantages is they
tended not to include me in the real
troublesome stuff. I was on the outside of that.

♦

It was not an environment to be ashamed of, but
growing up there proved that it is possible to
rise above conditions.

I had a great childhood. I had a close family, which provided everything I needed.

♦

People [hung] out of windows, watching. We didn't call it a neighborhood watch back then. We just called it hanging out the window. . . . It wasn't perfect. We had violence. We had drugs. A lot of kids did not get off that block, but I did and others of my friends did.

♦

My first early memories are of World War II. I was four when that war started and nine when it ended. At the age of thirteen, the Korean War broke out, and when [it] ended I was graduating from high school. So for a large part of my school days the nation was at war.

I didn't do [drugs]. Never in my life, not even to experiment, not to try, not to see what it would be like, for two reasons. One, my parents would have killed me, but the second reason is that somewhere along the line . . . we knew it was stupid. It was stupid. It was the most self-destructive thing you could do with the life that God and your parents had given to you.

♦

[For my first job at a bottler], the bottling machine caught my eye, but only the white boys worked there. I was hired as a porter. I decided to be the best mop wielder there ever was. It was almost more than I could bear. But I kept on mopping. At summer's end, the foreman said, 'You mop floors pretty good.' I said, 'You sure gave me enough opportunity to learn, sir.' Next summer he put me to work loading bottles. The third summer, I was deputy foreman.

♦

I remember, upon occasion, experiencing the feeling 'you can't make it.' When I was coming up, opportunities were limited. But now the opportunities are there to be anything you want to be.

On Affirmative Action

I benefitted from affirmative action in the Army, not because I was a quota promotion or because someone said he's black move him ahead. I benefitted from affirmative action in the Army because the Army said we're all going to be equal and if anybody needs a little bit more help to be equal, we're going to give them that help.

♦

Why shouldn't a group of senior officials in a university take a look at the total background of these youngsters? That's what they claim they do. They claim they just don't let them in on the basis of the SAT scores. They let them in on the basis of the hardships they've had to overcome, what they will contribute to the student body, whether their parents might have gone to that particular university. Let's get rid of that preference, whether they play ball well, and that'll also lend itself to scholarships. But what we shouldn't do is say we're going to have six blacks or because you're black, you're coming in. Look at the total student. See what is best for the community.

♦

It's amazing how affirmative action has suddenly become Issue No. 1. One of my Republican friends had the nerve to send me one of their newsletters a few weeks ago saying that we had to get rid of affirmative action because we couldn't keep putting these programs in place for allegations of 'vague and ancient wrongs.' I almost went crazy. Denny's wouldn't serve four black Secret Service agents guarding the President of the United States. . . . Don't throw out the baby with the bathwater.

♦

I'm a great believer in affirmative action and equal opportunity. I've seen it work in the military. What we've been able to achieve in the military is an open society where you can rise by performance, but if you have some weaknesses to begin with, through outreach programs, through remedial programs, we bring you up to a certain level of standard so you can compete.

On Gun Control

I am a gun owner. I firmly believe in the Second Amendment right to bear arms. I have rifles, pistols and shotguns. But at the same time, I am willing to put up with some level of inconvenience in acquiring guns or having guns in my possession that makes sure that I am a responsible citizen who should be allowed to have a gun.

On Drugs

I've been very outspoken on drugs. I tell lots of stories about how we deal with drugs in the military through testing and through a zero-tolerance attitude, which we can do in the military. I'm not sure you can do it in a school system somewhere in one of our big cities.

◆

I was preparing for my new responsibilities as Chairman when . . . a lieutenant appeared in the doorway and said my name had come up for random testing for drug abuse—a urinalysis. He didn't care if I was going to be the Chairman of the Joint Chiefs of Staff. . . . He was there with his kit and his rubber gloves. As you can see, I passed. That's the kind of approach you have to take to drugs.

On His Personal Life

General Harry Homeowner. *(What he calls himself living in a $1.3 million mansion after years of Army housing)*

♦

Most of my leisure time is spent at home. We are not big vacation people. I like movies, American Movie Classics. I like comedy. I watch a lot of news. I read a lot. My wife and I spend a lot of time together with our children and grandchildren.

On Free Speech

We had some people who came by [the book signing] to express their views [on abortion] to me. And I thought it was their role to do so.

♦

On Welfare Reform

I don't really know enough about welfare to comment on whether one senator or the other is right. I think something has to be done about the welfare program. It is not achieving its original purpose.

♦

As I listen to the debate over unwed mothers, I go past that to the child. I realize there is a need to make sure that the government is not in some way encouraging people to have children just to get another $80 or $90 a month.

♦

On Being a Public Figure

[It's] not foreign to me. I've been in the public eye for eight years. So this doesn't trouble me. I'm used to being misunderstood, taken out of context, attacked, so it's something I can endure.

♦

On Children

[Our problems will be solved by] parents bringing into the world a desired child, a child to be loved, to be nurtured, to be given a sense of what is right and wrong, to be prepared to enter a school system and be educated and made ready to enter a land of opportunity that we are blessed stewards of—a land that we are proud to call America.

♦

That's what children get from their parents: what they see. Not lectures or speeches. Children watch the way their parents live their lives. If they like what they see, if it makes sense to them, they will live their lives that way, too.

♦

Aren't these supposed to be the clumsy, lazy, dumb, untrainable, drugged-up teenagers that aren't ready for the future? Only if you let them.

On Dealing with the Media

Why do I have to talk to these people every week? All they ever want to know is who did what to whom. They never ask about substance.

Every pore in my face shows. *(Powell on a cover photo of him)*

♦

You can win the battle or lose the war if you don't handle the story right.

♦

You can't show your hole card, and if you go and bared your soul, the press would rip you apart.

♦

I have always tilted toward the black media. I've made myself very accessible to the black press and I do that as a way of just showing people, 'Hey, look at that dude. He came out of the South Bronx. If he got out, why can't I?'

You can't underestimate the importance of
dealing with the press and media in shaping
foreign policy. . . . I'm not talking about spin
control, I'm not talking about deception. I'm just
talking about . . . being accessible to the press,
realizing that they have a job to do, not being
afraid of them, not looking down on them, but
just working with them.

◆

CNN can show, within 15 minutes, the dead
body, the grieving mother . . . and the wife who's
going to sue you.

◆

A major barf. *(Powell on the fawning cover story
about him in the July 10 issue of* Time *magazine)*

I was going to be more candid and going to talk more about black youngsters in a white world, [but] I have to be careful. *(Powell's response when C-SPAN unexpectedly showed up to tape his talk)*

On the Religious Right

I am troubled by the political passion of those on the extreme right who seem to claim divine wisdom on political as well as spiritual matters. I am disturbed by the class and racial overtones beneath the surface of their rhetoric.

On Liberals

I am put off by patronizing liberals who claim to know what is best for society but devote little thought to who will eventually pay the bills.

On Fidel Castro

He is the Gloria Swanson of world leaders.
Castro, a pathetic, irrelevant, aging starlet, still
shows up for casting calls, carrying faded, dog-
eared 8-by-10 glossies, and accompanied by a
crew of bodyguards that needs 10 tons of
weapons to feel secure.

On America's Reputation Abroad

We have a very bad reputation around the world
now as an incontinent political entity. And it's
hurt the President badly and his statesmanship
really badly. But what are the long-term
consequences?

On President Bill Clinton

[I'm] not a fan of the manner in which foreign policy issues are hammered out in this administration . . . [There's] too much tactical judging from day to day and week to week.

♦

I would never answer a question like that; it is so hypothetical. George Bush served his nation with great distinction for many years. He lost the election of 1992. Bill Clinton is now our President. He will stand on his record next year. *(Powell responding to a charge that his vote for Bush in 1992 means that he condemns Clinton today)*

I visit with him regularly. He sends me off to strange and wondrous places from time to time.

♦

[I have] doubts about some of his habits.

On an Independent Party

[It would] throw some more fun into the race.

♦

I think there is probably greater support for an independent movement than there was a year ago. That's reflected in all the polling. It is not clear yet whether an independent run, unless it is self-financed, can actually succeed in winning a general election and winning the electoral college. . . . [This] reflects more dissatisfaction in the countryside with what they see the two parties doing.

On College

I went to college for a single reason: my parents expected it. I don't recall having had any great urge to get a higher education.

♦

I really don't know if I would have finished
college if it had not been for the ROTC
program.

♦

[College] had provided me with an appreciation
of the liberal arts; it had given me an insight
into the fundamentals of government; and it had
given me a deep respect for our democratic
system.

♦

[The City College of New York] represented an
unwritten but intuitively understood three-way
bargain—that the kids would work hard, the
parents would support them, and the schools
would teach them.

Today I have several children who don't think that the end of college is necessarily the beginning of a productive work life. But we're sorting it out, each child at a time.

On His Values

I sometimes think that I'm probably sounding a little too corny, a little too preachy. But then I realize that all I'm talking about are values, values that I was raised with, that you were probably raised with, that are traditional American values. . . . Even if it is corny, it's still valuable to hear. It's good stuff.

◆

On Whites

A lot of white people salve their consciences by saying, 'Well, look, we've got a Colin Powell, and he's not a basketball player. They can do it.' And so they cop out. . . . However many white people use me as a cover for their conscience, I assume at least ten times as many black people are gaining some inspiration from me.

◆

On Conservative Republicans

[They have put] energy back into our political system. I support a lot of what they are suggesting—less government, seeing what we can do about bringing our entitlements, taxes and deficit under control.

♦

"Can you imagine me standing up and talking to these people?" Powell asked.

"Yes," Batjer [his former assistant] replied, knowing his adaptability.

"Who needs it?" Powell said.

♦

On Jesse Jackson

While I was comfortably ensconced in the government bureaucracy enjoying civil rights, Jesse was out there fighting, and I appreciate that. All I can do is continue to present myself as I see myself and let others make judgments.

On Taxes

Nobody should want to raise taxes. I mean this is part of the Republican side of my brain. But you can't make that claim at the same time that we're also running horrible deficits. Somehow it has to be brought into balance.

On Being a Private Person

I'm a very private person, and my family is a private existence. We live quiet and private lives. So [running for office] would be a change in the life of my family unlike anything we have ever experienced before. And I have to give very, very serious thought about whether we should do that to the family.

◆

I thoroughly enjoy being private, going to the store with no guards, no chauffeur, no beeper.

◆

While I am going out to acquire something of a private life again and spend more time with my family and get off stage for a while, I think in due course I would like to be seen as serving the nation in some way.

◆

I love it. I really like doing this. *(Powell on cleaning the grout between the tiles of his kitchen floor)*

◆

On Patriotism

I tell you if that doesn't make your heart go pitty-pat, you ought to lie down and get someone to throw some dirt on you, 'cause you're dead. *(On hearing "God Bless the USA" sung at a seminar where he spoke)*

On Public Programs

Our leaders [must be] willing to talk straight to the American people about Medicare and Social Security.

♦

Is there really that much difference between what the Clinton administration wants to do with Medicare and what the Republicans on the Hill want to do with Medicare? Do they both want to cut it? Yes. So what's the fight?

◆

As I go around the country I sense that the American people want to see [cuts] done with some level of compassion. They realize that we have to look at these programs, but we don't want to do it in such a harsh way that some of our fellow citizens who are in greatest need are not taken care of.

◆

On the Vietnam War

The parades and celebrations are not needed to restore our honor as Vietnam veterans because we never lost our honor. They're not to clear up the matter of our valor because our valor was never in question.

♦

I was an infantry officer, and I was very excited about going. It was what infantry officers should want to do. So I not only had no reservations about it, I was looking forward to it. I was twenty-four years old or something. It was hot stuff.

♦

We bombed the hell out of Vietnam and never did stop anything on the Ho Chi Minh Trail.

On the Army

The Army has been my home. The Army has been my life. The Army has been my profession. The Army has been my love for all these many years. I am what I am today, because the Army takes care of its own.

◆

Soldiering is about people in the same value system, the same cultural system. You go from one Army post to another, you might as well have been at the last one. You immediately fit in.

I wish that there were other activities in our society and in our nation that were as open as the military is to upward mobility, to achievement, to allowing them in.

◆

I believe that military service to the nation is an honorable profession and a contribution to society.

◆

You've got to see our force as a human, living organism and treat it as such.

◆

I threw the bums out of the Army and put the drug users in jail. The rest, we ran four miles every morning, and by night they were too tired to get into trouble. *(Powell's strategy on working with a troubled infantry unit in Korea in 1973)*

◆

The military has done a tremendous job in integrating its forces.

◆

I think by the middle '80s . . . the American people started to sense that, hey, maybe these folks are quite good. Maybe their leaders are reasonably competent. Maybe it isn't as bad as people have been telling us.

The fact that we have a higher percentage [of blacks] than the percentage that exists in the general population doesn't trouble me at all. That's why I came in. To get a job. $222.30 a month.

♦

The Army has always been exposed to the tensions of society. . . . Our challenge was to melt that all out and reduce it to just soldiers dressed in green uniforms all equal, all sharing, all ready to sacrifice for each other.

♦

When I came along in 1958, I was able to
capture all of what was done before by men in
segregated units denied the opportunity to
advance. They had the potential as I might have
had. It's different now, but . . . we cannot let the
torch drop.

◆

Every year your armed forces creates [a strong]
bonding among about three hundred thousand
young men and women who come in and who
leave. Young whites who go back to their homes
all over this country having been family with
young blacks. And young blacks who go back to
their homes all over this country having been
treated as an equal brother with their white
colleagues.

In the old days, the Army said, 'If we had wanted you to have a wife, we'd have issued you one.' That mentality went out with the volunteer Army. We have to keep a family happy to keep a soldier serving.

On Writing His Book

I am going to write a book because I have some things I want to say, some thoughts I want to pass on. I have had a wonderful life. I've had a great experience in the military, and I want to put my side down on a number of the issues I've been involved in over the years.

♦

[My editors] told me I had to stop sanding it . . . but I thought it might be too long.

◆

[It was] like connecting the dots of your life. It was very introspective for me and I came away with a deeper appreciation of my own family roots, but an even greater appreciation of the nation we live in.

◆

You're never done [writing a book]. I hate this profession. I am an amateur, and I am leaving the profession.

◆

On Getting Things Done

I only have to do so much compromising. There comes a time when I can just say, 'Do it!'

◆

I have an insatiable demand to be in charge of the information flow. If you don't know what information is flowing through your organization, you don't know what's going on in your organization.

◆

I have not allowed myself to be coerced . . . to provide very, very cheap [solutions] that look neat but won't accomplish the intended purpose.

On the Use of Military Force

We go, we win.

♦

You don't bomb people for credibility. We have repeatedly gotten in trouble thinking that the use of military force is for the purpose of being seen as having done something. You should use military force for achieving a specific military purpose that is linked to the achievement of a specific political purpose and goal.

♦

The use of force is ultimately a political act, not a military act.

♦

The constant must be to ensure that our armed forces always remain good, that they always have what is needed to accomplish their mission, that they are never asked to respond to the call of an uncertain trumpet.

♦

We are not committing mercenaries. We are committing sons and daughters.

♦

Many experts, amateurs and others in this town believe that [forcing Iraq out of Kuwait] can be accomplished by such things as surgical air strikes, or perhaps a sustained air strike. . . . Those strategies may work, but they also may not. Such strategies are designed to *hope* to win, they are not designed to win.

◆

Peace through strength vanishes as a possibility if there is no strength.

◆

I believe in the bully's way of going to war. 'I'm on the street corner, I got my gun, I got my blade, *I'ma kick yo' ass.*'

If we listened to some military men, there would never be a step toward peace.

◆

Don't count on the easy ways. You can't put a ship in the gulf and lob shells and do anything.

◆

We do deserts, not mountains.

◆

My own view is that if there's going to be a war, if the American people know that we have been committed to it, they will want it done quickly, decisively and with as few casualties as possible.

◆

If we're going to have a military presence, it ought to be a force that looks like it can fight.

♦

If you finally decide you have to commit military force, you've got to be as massive and decisive as possible. Decide your target, decide your objective, and try to overwhelm it.

♦

On Foreign Policy

We have to have an adequate level of strategic nuclear power, offensive power, to deter the Soviet Union. . . . They still have twenty-seven thousand nuclear weapons in that land of eleven time zones. . . . I will never allow the strategic nuclear forces of the United States to ever be second best to any nation that has similar weapons which can destroy our way of life in thirty minutes. That's a given.

♦

I think it is very, very useful for world peace and in order to steer ourselves into the future we're all hoping for, for the United States to be seen as a very powerful nation—politically powerful because of our value system, economically powerful, and, yes, militarily powerful. I don't think we should apologize for that.

♦

We've heard it again and again: America cannot be the world's policeman. Yet . . . when there's trouble, when somebody needs a cop, who gets called to restore peace? We do.

♦

The wake-up call can come at any moment, and we don't put our friends and interests on hold.

The debates that we're seeing now about unilateralism or multilateralism or isolationism and interventionism and the other 'isms' are somewhat silly and they miss the point. The point is that history and destiny have made America the leader of the world that would be free. And the world that would be free is looking to us for inspiration.

♦

On President Ronald Reagan

The problem with Reagan and Bush is that they never knew [about racism]. . . . They never had to live with it. . . . This was an area where I found them wanting. . . . Just read it [a photograph of Reagan on which the president had written 'If you say so, Colin, it must be right']. And so now I'm going to turn around and say he's a racist?

♦

A genius.

♦

Reagan himself is color-blind, but he bears a responsibility for being blind to the impact of what his administration has not done for black people.

♦

I had trouble [writing] the Reagan chapters because I have a loving relationship with him and had to be honest without being hurtful.

On President George Bush

[Brent Scowcroft was] First Companion and all-purpose playmate to the President on golf, fishing, and weekend outings.

♦

My beloved friend.

[We get along] great. He comes by here every day for around 15 minutes and schmoozes.

On the Gulf War

Our strategy to go after this army is very, very simple. First we're going to cut it off, and then we're going to kill it.

♦

We got enough force in there to let [Saddam Hussein] know he was pulling on Superman's cape and he better stop.

♦

No Iraqi leader should think for a moment that we don't have the will or ability to accomplish what might be required of us.

I have to keep reminding people: I was just an adviser. I owed my bosses my best insight—and then I owed them my total loyalty for whatever they decided to do.

♦

Guilty. War is a deadly game. *(Powell's response to a statement that he was a "reluctant warrior" in the war)*

♦

Trust me. *(His plea during the Gulf War)*

♦

The first [war] in history to be interrupted for Zamfir commercials.

We dropped a lot of dumb bombs in Desert Storm. We've done it in every war. The reason you drop lots of them is that you're hoping through the laws of statistics and probability one of them is going to hit your target.

◆

When we had kicked the Iraqi army out of Kuwait, I had no reservations and will never have any reservations about having been part of a decision process with President Bush that said, 'Let's stop killing people.' . . . Iraqis have parents, too.

On North Korea

If we ever think that [North Korea] is going to use [a nuclear bomb], or if [they] do use one, [they]'ll become a charcoal briquette.

On Democracy

'All kinds of politicians. They give speeches, and they shout and scream and they are reactionary and liars and thieves and crooks and criminals,' [say the Russian generals who seek Powell's advice on democracy]. And I say, 'Welcome to democracy, babe! It's just like Washington. That's what it's all about. You're going to learn to live with it, and you're going to love it.'

♦

Have faith in our political system, which is unlike any other in the world.

♦

On What He Likes to Be Called

Everybody around here calls me *Co*-lin; my family called me *Cah*-lin. I don't like the damned name anyway, so call me what you like.

◆

His "Rules"

1. It ain't as bad as you think. It will look better in the morning.
2. Get mad, then get over it.
3. Avoid having your ego so close to your position that, when your position falls, your ego goes with it.

4. It can be done!

5. Be careful what you choose. You may get it.

6. Don't let adverse facts stand in the way of a good decision.

7. You can't make someone else's choices. You shouldn't let someone else make yours.

8. Check small things.

9. Share credit.

10. Remain calm. Be kind.

11. Have a vision. Be demanding.

12. Don't take counsel of your fears or naysayers.

13. Perpetual optimism is a force multiplier.

On His Critics

[William] Safire drives me to distraction. Sometimes, because he starts down this logic trail, and every time he gets trapped he just says, 'Air power can do it.' Forget it. The technology isn't that good. . . . Bullshit, Bill. But he does that. He's getting increasingly arrogant in his old age.

♦

The last person in the world I feel a need to defend my courage to is Senator [Alphonse] D'Amato. *(Powell responding to a barb by the Senator)*

◆

People sometimes say, well, Powell, he's a political general anyway. The fact of the matter is there isn't a general in Washington who isn't political, not if he's going to be successful, because that's the nature of our system.

◆

On Bosnia

The biggest mistake was recognizing all these
little countries when they started to decide they
were independent. The Serbs had very good
reason to be worried about being in a Muslim-
dominated country. It wasn't just paranoia.
When the fighting broke out, should the West
have intervened militarily as one of the
belligerents to put down all other belligerents?
There was no Western leader who was willing to
say, 'I have a vital interest in the outcome of
this conflict.' Nobody really thinks it has a vital
interest.

♦

This isn't like Desert Storm. You have hills, you have trees. You have a civilian population, you have churches, you have homes, you have schools, and they can park all that artillery right next to any of that stuff, and you can't bomb it.

♦

I think you ought to send a clear signal: that we're not going to get involved in this war, and it's not going to end until people are tired of fighting one another. If you say that every day, the Muslims will know it and the Serbs will know it, and there will be no confusion.

♦

On the Vice-Presidency

I'm known to be a rather cautious person, and I always like to preserve all options to the very end, and so I would never rule anything out prematurely, but at the moment [the vice-presidency] is not something that appeals to me.

♦

The theory behind it is: God, why would anybody want to be the Vice-President? The [combining two jobs of] Secretary of State–Vice-President idea is a way of taking away some of the misery of being Vice-President, which puts you in hiding somewhere. They park you for four years. I think there's a problem. I don't think you can do two jobs well at the same time, and there *is* a job for the Vice-President.

114

On What the Government Can Do

I don't know how to write a federal program telling two people to fall in love and stay together.

On His Views

I am not an ideologue.

◆

I'm principally a broker. I have strong views on things, but my job is to make sure the president gets the best information available to make an informed decision. *(Talking about his job as national security adviser)*

115

The rule I follow was given to me by one of my mentors, Charles Duncan. When I told him something awful had happened, he said, 'Well, Colin, if all else fails and we have no choice, tell the truth.'

On Gays

I never presented the case in terms of there being something wrong, morally, or any other way, with gays [in the military]. I just couldn't figure out a way to handle the privacy aspect.

♦

[The American family] doesn't even have to be a two-gender family.

On His Career

I was told, 'If you do everything well and keep your nose clean for twenty years, we'll make you a lieutenant colonel.' That was my goal.

◆

My career has [followed] a weird career pattern. The army does not write it up and send it out as an example!

◆

Alma, we're moving again. (*Upon being selected by President Bush to be Chairman of the Joint Chiefs of Staff*)

◆

I didn't refuse this job [as national security adviser], but neither did I go out looking for it.

◆

My ambitions, such that they were, were much more modest [during ROTC]. They were simply to get out of New York, get a job and go out and have some excitement. At that time I never even thought seriously about staying in the Army.

◆

If [Reagan] wants me, then I have to do it.

◆

I figured I could make it in the military.

I've been a soldier all my life. I've never wanted
to be anything else.

◆

[I feel] privileged to be the first black person to
hold this senior White House position.

◆

There were other opportunities, making a lot
more money than I am now. Every time I have
faced up to this choice, I just find the
satisfaction of being a soldier and the love of my
profession overwhelming and more important to
me than making a great deal of money or doing
something I may not like as much as being a
soldier.

I think my life would be incomplete if I was not serving the nation and our society in some way. Everybody wants to talk about politics, but I believe there are other ways to serve the nation than embarking on a political career.

♦

Reasons to stay in the Army: One dozen. Reasons to leave the Army: One—money. *(A list Powell made in 1988 before taking over the Army's biggest single command, in Atlanta)*

♦

I feel, just as an American citizen, and because of the position I have reached, I think there will be an obligation on me to do something in public life.

120

I think people have been generally pleased by the way the military has performed during recent crises, and so they think that is instantly transferable into a civilian political environment. I'm not sure it really is.

◆

[I follow a strategy with] the highest potential for success and entails the least possible risk.

◆

I am feeling older every year, every day, but I'm not exactly the Ancient Mariner yet. And I suspect I have another 15 years of service.

◆

I ain't done bad.

I want to keep my options open. I'm going to do something to try to help make this an even greater country than it is now. Just keep watching. I'll be out there somewhere.

On His Celebrity Status

[General Norman Schwarzkopf and I were] leaders who seemed to be reasonably intelligent, reasonably articulate . . . [we] were not a bunch of Dr. Strangeloves.

On the Contract with America

Some parts I find a little too hard, a little too harsh, a little too unkind. We do not yet have a level playing field in our society.

On Women in Combat

Because of the close nature of those operations and the kind of bonding you need in units of that kind, they really have to be all male, in my judgment.

On Haiti

I treated [the Haitian generals] as soldiers. And Raoul Cedras responded as a soldier. He said there would be no resistance, and he said it in such a way, with such confidence, that I knew he meant it. So we were able to go forward.

♦

On Retirement

I don't want to spend the rest of my life giving speeches.

♦

The Army has officially advised me that, for record purposes, I have served 35 years, 3 months, 21 days, and, as we say in the infantry, a wake-up. I loved every single day of it. And it's hard to leave.

♦

On the Secret of Success

The core is putting people—youngsters—into
the kind of arrangement I had as a youngster.
Two parents who loved me, who could provide a
home for me, who could give me some structure
and discipline in my life.

◆

There are no secrets to success; don't waste time
looking for them. Success is the result of
perfection, hard work, learning from failure,
loyalty to those for whom you work, and
persistence.

◆

On Sex Education

[They're] exposed to contraception, but the first thing they do is just: 'Listen—abstinence. You're too young to have sex with a boy. Here's why you don't have to do it. Here's how you tell them no, and here's why you have to tell them no.'

◆

On the Constitution

The U.S. Constitution is a remarkable document—and a demanding one for those of us who choose to make our career in the military. We are required to pledge our sacred honor to a document that looks at the military . . . as a necessary, but undesirable, institution useful in times of crisis; and to be watched carefully at all other times.

◆

I hate fooling with the Constitution.

◆

On Young People in America

All you have to do is send this major and a couple of sergeants into a school anywhere and put some uniforms on these kids; that's structure. You put them all in a uniform, they all look alike. That takes care of the Nikes, it takes care of all the fancy clothes, it takes care of all the other crap we're wasting money on our kids with.

♦

They have got to prepare themselves. They have got to be ready. . . . Now that I am on top of that cliff looking ahead, there are still some more hurdles to be crossed, and our young people have to be ready.

[We give them] some structure, expectations, caring, role modeling, recognition, reward, punishment—meaning there are consequences for poor behavior and not meeting standards. And then all the help in the world to meet those standards.

◆

I feel an obligation to help young people, especially minority young people.

◆

On Whether He'll Run for President

I'll sit down with my family and those people who provide me with advice and counsel and some very dear friends who care about me and make a decision as to what to do with the next phase of my life.

♦

People say, 'Well, what do you expect to happen one morning? You suddenly have the pilot light that sets off the boilers?' I don't know what might or might not happen. . . . If I really think I have something to offer, and believe that I can offer it in a way that no one else can, and it's something that the American people are responsive to, then it wouldn't surprise me if I reached that point and the boilers went off.

♦

Now, there's another thing that nobody recommends. But I have to think about it: I'm only going to be sixty-three in 1999—nine years younger than Dole is now.

♦

I advance with obedience to the work, ready to retire from it whenever you become sensible how much better choice it is in your power to make. *(Citing Thomas Jefferson's first inaugural address in response to questions about whether he'll run)*

♦

What you're going to hear for the next few weeks is what I think and what I believe. I am in one of the best positions I will ever be in. I am free to say what I believe. I'll speak out from my heart and experience.

♦

Time will run out on me in the fall, and I will have to make a decision. And so the book tour is an important part of this.

♦

The book tour will give me some indication of what I'll have to put up with as a political figure. And when I come off that, then I will do an analysis of what it really requires, and whether I have a vision that is sufficiently different from the vision that's out there. And then Alma and I will sit down. And then one night my instinct will take over and say, 'This is what I want.'

♦

I have no political ambitions at the moment, Mr.
Donaldson. I just want to be the best chairman
I can be.

◆

I have no political aspirations at the moment. I
don't know that it's required of me to say what I
might do when I'm seventy-five years old.

◆

I plan to vote, yeah. *(Powell's response to a
student's query on Powell's plans to participate
in presidential politics in 1996)*

◆

On America Today

I'm very mindful today that the period we are entering may be the most historic period in the postwar era. It will be a time of hope, a time of opportunity, a time of anxiety, of instability, of uncertainty, and yes, a time of risk and danger. But we are not afraid of the future. We enter this era secure in knowing who we are and what we stand for.

◆

Sources

Time magazine, September 18, 1995

The Washington Post Magazine, September 24, 1995

Time magazine, July 10, 1995

20/20 with Barbara Walters

Time magazine, September 18, 1995

Time magazine, July 10, 1995

New York Times, September 29, 1993

Newsweek, May 13, 1991

U.S. News & World Report, September 20, 1993

Time magazine, September 18, 1995

Chicago Sun-Times, September 22, 1995

New York Times, January 31, 1995

Newsweek, September 11, 1995

U.S. News & World Report, March 18, 1991

New York Times, January 31, 1995

The New Yorker, "Powell and the Black Elite," by Henry Louis Gates, Jr., September 25, 1995

New York Times, January 31, 1995

The New Yorker, September 25, 1995

New York Times, September 29, 1993

New York Times, January 31, 1995

The New Yorker, September 25, 1995

Time magazine, September 11, 1995

New York Times, January 31, 1995

Powell for President! web page

20/20 with Barbara Walters

The New Yorker, September 25, 1995

The New Yorker, September 25, 1995

Colin Powell: A Biography, by Howard Means,
   published in hardcover by Donald I. Fine, 1992;
   reprinted in paperback by Ballantine Books, 1993;
   page 36

From a speech at Morris High School, the Bronx,
   April 1991, in *Colin Powell: A Biography*, page 32

Colin Powell: A Biography, page 36

Time magazine, September 18, 1995

Time magazine, September 18, 1995

The New Yorker, September 25, 1995

Speech from National School Boards Association
   conference, 1995

20/20 with Barbara Walters

20/20 with Barbara Walters

Chicago Sun-Times, September 22, 1995

Time magazine, July 10, 1995

Time magazine, September 11, 1995

National Review, April 1, 1991

Black Collegian, April 1991, in *Colin Powell: A Biography*, page 148

Speech at Fisk University, May 4, 1992, in *Colin Powell: A Biography*, page 37

Newsweek, September 3, 1990

Colin Powell: A Biography, page 89

Speech to Tuskegee Airmen, February 1991, in *Colin Powell: A Biography*, page 90

Ebony, July 1988

Time magazine, July 10, 1995

Vanity Fair, October 1995

Newsweek, September 11, 1995

Washington Post, in *Colin Powell: A Biography*, page 120

The New Yorker, September 25, 1995

Reuter's, September 25, 1995

The Washington Monthly, December 1994

Reuter's, September 25, 1995

Reuter's, September 25, 1995

The Washington Monthly, December 1994

The New Yorker, September 25, 1995

Colin Powell: A Biography, page 16

Colin Powell: A Biography, page 16

The New Republic, May 30, 1988

At a national convention of the Tuskegee Airmen,
    August 1991, in *Colin Powell: A Biography*, page
    16

National Review, April 1, 1991

The Washingtonian, in *Colin Powell: A Biography*,
    page 24

Newsweek, October 10, 1994

Parade magazine, in *Colin Powell: A Biography*, page
    63

Sunday Gleaner magazine, 1988, in *Colin Powell: A
    Biography*, page 25

The Public Interest, Winter 1989

Colin Powell: A Biography, page 26

Colin Powell: A Biography, page 64

Colin Powell: A Biography, page 26

The New Republic, May 30, 1988

Parade magazine, in *Colin Powell: A Biography*, page
    26

Colin Powell: A Biography, page 27

The New Republic, May 30, 1988

National Review, April 1, 1991

People magazine, Special Issue, Spring/Summer 1991

Time magazine, July 10, 1995

The Washingtonian, in *Colin Powell: A Biography*,
    page 47

Vanity Fair, October 1995

Newsweek, September 11, 1995

Chicago Sun-Times, September 22, 1995

Chicago Sun-Times, September 22, 1995

The New Yorker, September 25, 1995

Ebony, February 1990

Time magazine, July 10, 1995

Time magazine, September 18, 1995

New York Times, October 1, 1995

The Washington Post Magazine, September 24, 1995

The New Yorker, September 25, 1995

Colin Powell: A Biography, page 159–160

The New Yorker, September 25, 1995

U.S. News & World Report, September 20, 1993

New York Times, September 24, 1995

CNN, September 9, 1995

The New Yorker, September 25, 1995

The New Yorker, September 25, 1995

U.S. News & World Report, September 20, 1993

U.S. News & World Report, September 20, 1993

Parade magazine, in *Colin Powell: A Biography*, page 123

U.S. News & World Report, September 20, 1993

Ebony, February 1990

The Washingtonian, in *Colin Powell: A Biography*,
  page 146

The Washingtonian, in *Colin Powell: A Biography*,
  page 248

The Washingtonian, in *Colin Powell: A Biography*,
  page 146

The Washingtonian, in Colin Powell: A Biography,
  page 216

The Washington Monthly, December 1994

The Washington Monthly, December 1994

Houston Chronicle, September 27, 1995

New Hampshire Sunday News, October 8, 1995, from
  an interview with *The Rocky Mountain News*,
  October 4, 1995

From a 1995 speech at Lawson State
  Community College, in *The Atlantic*, October 1993

Ebony, February 1990

WBUR, Boston, September 24, 1995

People magazine, October 2, 1995

National Review, April 1, 1991

Colin Powell: A Biography, page 15

People magazine, October 2, 1995

Hunts Point and Southern Boulevard Observer, 1989,
  in *Colin Powell: A Biography*, page 38

The Washingtonian, in *Colin Powell: A Biography*,
  page 41

Sources

Ebony, July 1988

People magazine, September 10, 1990

Chicago Sun-Times, September 22, 1995

The Washingtonian, in *Colin Powell: A Biography*,
 page 43

Speech at Morris High School, the Bronx, April 1991,
 in *Colin Powell: A Biography*, page 47

Guideposts, November 1991, in *Colin Powell: A
 Biography*, page 48

Speech at Morris High School, the Bronx, April 1991,
 in *Colin Powell: A Biography*, page 33

20/20 with Barbara Walters

20/20 with Barbara Walters

The New Yorker, September 25, 1995

Reuter's, September 25, 1995

20/20 with Barbara Walters

U.S. News & World Report, September 20, 1993

Colin Powell: A Biography, page 35–36

Time magazine, March 10, 1995

Chicago Sun-Times, September 22, 1995

San Jose Mercury News, September 18, 1995

20/20 with Barbara Walters

Time magazine, September 18, 1995

Time magazine, September 18, 1995

National School Boards Association conference, 1995

Parade magazine, in *Colin Powell: A Biography*, page 63–64

Colin Powell: A Biography, page 35

The New Republic, May 30, 1988

The Washington Post Magazine, September 24, 1995

U.S. News & World Report, September 20, 1993

The Washington Post Magazine, September 24, 1995

Ebony, February 1990

The Washington Post Magazine, September 24, 1995

Newsweek, October 10, 1994

The Washington Post Magazine, September 24, 1995

The Washington Post Magazine, September 24, 1995

Time magazine, September 11, 1995

Time magazine, September 11, 1995

The Washington Post Magazine, September 24, 1995

The New Yorker, September 25, 1995

20/20 with Barbara Walters

The Today Show

New York Times, January 31, 1995

Time magazine, October 3, 1994

Time magazine, March 10, 1995

Time magazine, September 18, 1995

The Public Interest, Winter 1989

The Washingtonian, in *Colin Powell: A Biography*, page 69

The Public Interest, Winter 1989

U.S. News & World Report, March 18, 1991

The Public Interest, Winter 1989

60 Minutes, in *Colin Powell: A Biography*, page 78

Colin Powell: A Biography, page 89

Reuter's, September 21, 1995

The Washington Post Magazine, September 24, 1995

Boston Globe, September 25, 1995

20/20 with Barbara Walters

Time magazine, September 18, 1995

People magazine, October 2, 1995

New York Times, September 12, 1993

The Washington Post Magazine, September 24, 1995

Vanity Fair, October 1995, on hearing "God Bless
   the USA" sung at a seminar where he spoke

Time magazine, July 10, 1995

Time magazine, September 18, 1995

Reuter's, September 21, 1995

Speech, Memorial Day 1991, at the Vietnam
   Veteran's Memorial, in *Colin Powell: A Biography*,
   page 294

The Washingtonian, in *Colin Powell: A Biography*,
   page 107

The New Yorker, September 25, 1995

The New Republic, April 17, 1995

U.S. News & World Report, September 20, 1993

Jet, March 4, 1991

The Public Interest, Winter 1989

New York Times, October 1, 1993

Reader's Digest, December 1989

Jet, September 11, 1989

U.S. News & World Report, September 20, 1993

Jet, March 4, 1991

Book of the Month Club News, November 1995

Ebony, July 1988

Colin Powell: A Biography, page 34

U.S. News & World Report, December 24, 1990

New York Times, September 12, 1993

Book of the Month Club News, November 1995

Reuter's, September 25, 1995

The Washington Post Magazine, September 24, 1995

U.S. News & World Report, September 20, 1993

U.S. News & World Report, April 25, 1988

U.S. News & World Report, September 20, 1993

New York magazine, June 10, 1991

The New Yorker, September 25, 1995

U.S. News & World Report, September 20, 1993

Ebony, February 1990

New York Times, September 29, 1993

The Washington Monthly, December 1994

Reader's Digest, December 1989

The New Yorker, September 25, 1995

Reader's Digest, December 1989

Newsweek, September 3, 1990

Newsweek, October 10, 1994

U.S. News & World Report, December 24, 1990

Jet, May 28, 1990

Newsweek, September 3, 1990

MacNeil/Lehrer Newshour, March 1992, in *Colin Powell: A Biography*, page 279

MacNeil/Lehrer Newshour, March 1992, in *Colin Powell: A Biography*, page 280

Colin Powell: A Biography, page 280–281

U.S. News & World Report, March 18, 1991

New York Times, September 29, 1993

The New Yorker, September 25, 1995

New York Times, September 24, 1994

The Washington Post Magazine, September 24, 1995

The New Yorker, September 25, 1995

Newsweek, May 13, 1991

New York Times, September 24, 1994

Newsweek, May 13, 1991

Press conference, January 23, 1991, during the Gulf War

People magazine, Special Issue, Spring/Summer 1991

Newsweek, September 3, 1990

Newsweek, October 10, 1994

Newsweek, September 11, 1995

U.S. News & World Report, February 4, 1991

Newsweek, October 10, 1994

U.S. News & World Report, September 20, 1993

New York Times, January 31, 1995

New York Times, January 31, 1995

New York Times, January 31, 1995

From a speech at Lawson State Community College, reported in *The Atlantic*, October 1993

Vanity Fair, October 1995

Colin Powell: A Biography, page 197

The New Yorker, September 25, 1995

20/20 with Barbara Walters

The Washington Post Magazine, September 24, 1995

The New Yorker, September 25, 1995

The New Yorker, September 25, 1995

The New Yorker, September 25, 1995

In an interview with David Frost on a BBC program

The New Yorker, September 25, 1995

Chicago Sun-Times, September 22, 1995

The New Republic, May 30, 1988

The New Republic, May 30, 1988

National Review, April 1, 1991

The New Yorker, September 25, 1995

New York Times, January 31, 1995

National Review, April 1, 1991

Book of the Month Club News, November 1995

Reader's Digest, December 1989

National Review, April 1, 1991

Ebony, February 1990

Reader's Digest, December 1989

Ebony, July 1988

New York Times, September 29, 1993

Ebony, July 1988

C-Span, April 1992, in *Colin Powell: A Biography*,
   page 284

C-Span, April 1992, in *Colin Powell: A Biography*,
   page 286

Reader's Digest, December 1989

New York Times, September 12, 1993

C-Span, April 1992, in *Colin Powell: A Biography*,
   page 286

New York Times, May 26, 1995

U.S. News & World Report, September 20, 1993

Jet, March 4, 1991

New York Times, May 26, 1995

Book of the Month Club News, November 1995

New York Times, May 26, 1995

New York Times, September 29, 1993

Newsweek, October 10, 1994

New York Times, September 12, 1993

New York Times, October 1, 1993

Chicago Sun-Times, September 22, 1995

Ebony, July 1988

Chicago Sun-Times, September 22, 1995

U.S. News & World Report, February 4, 1991

New York Times, January 31, 1995

U.S. News & World Report, September 20, 1993

Jet, September 11, 1989

U.S. News & World Report, September 20, 1993

New York Times, September 12, 1993

Time magazine, September 18, 1995

Chicago Sun-Times, September 22, 1995

The New Yorker, September 25, 1995

Time magazine, September 18, 1995

U.S. News & World Report, February 4, 1991

The New Yorker, September 25, 1995

The New Yorker, September 25, 1995

Prime Time Live, July 1990

The Today Show, December 1991

60 Minutes, December 1991

Jet, October 23, 1989